The Squirrel
and the
Peanut Butter

B.I. Phillips

To order additional copies of this book, contact:
Xlibris
844-714-8691
www.Xlibris.com

ISBN: Softcover   978-1-6698-7038-8
        EBook   978-1-6698-7039-5

Print information available on the last page

Rev. date: 03/30/2023

This book belongs to:

_____

Grateful Acknowledgements:

USTA tennis and the Star Island Resort.

While perusing the USTA local tennis tournament schedule I came across a tournament in central Florida. I decided to enter. After paying my fee I eagerly awaited to see if I would be selected to play. Seeing that I was I waited to see what the organization of the tournament would be in terms of which opponents would play which opponents. Once securing my challengers in the tournament, I made note of the weather and what over the counter supplies I would need to play my best. Since it was summer and brutally hot I thought electrolytes would be a good choice. Having tried drinking products with electrolytes I thought tablets might be more efficient as they provided a dual function which was to reduce anxiety by keeping something in my mouth while playing.

Since I had no car due to a previous accident I figured out how seek and secure alternate transportation.

On the morning of the tournament I secured my alternate transportation and waited for them to arrive.

When my ride arrived it was a giant Lima bean so I wasn't sure.

So we set out for the tennis tournament.

When I arrived instead of the tournament director was a giant eggplant. I asked why were they handing out Brussel sprouts instead of tennis balls?

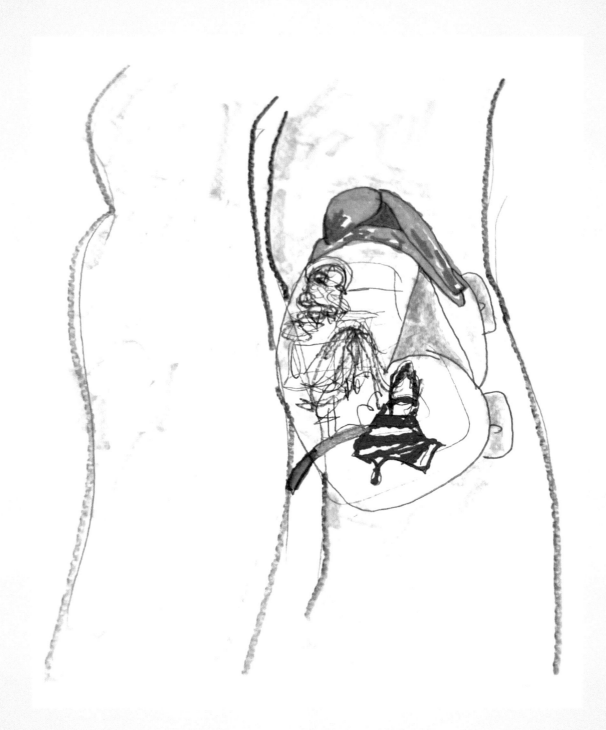

II

Remembering what my neighbor had told me "You don't ask." I took the Brussels sprouts and headed to the court. Being unable to concentrate I ask to move to another court. Magically upon resuming play on center court the Brussel sprouts turned back into tennis balls.

What happened next was beyond belief. In between serves I looked over to see a squirrel eating the peanut butter out of my jar.

The next thing I knew he was running off with the jar of peanut butter.

We continued with the match and discussed collegiate disciplines we both shared. Namely, chemistry and professors who or whom taught those disciplines currently and who was still there at USF.

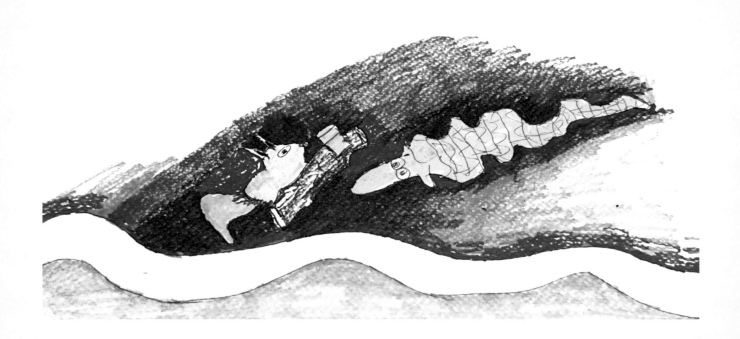

Little did I know the squirrel had gone to share the peanut butter with thumbs the alligator.

Hardly able to contain my excitement from the event I ran to tell the tournament director what we had seen. Having been told it happens all the time I felt deflated like the beach ball.

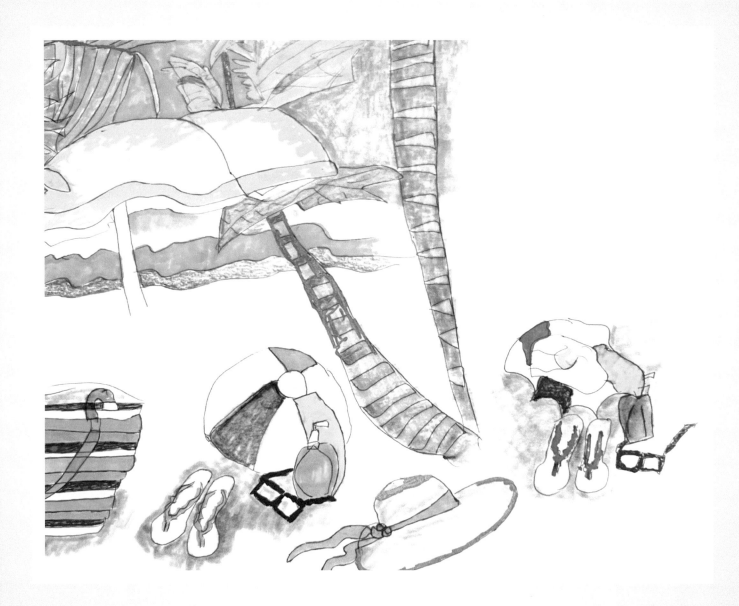

Well it was the first time something like this happened to me and I thought it was great!!!!

Finishing the match I went to talk to my friend Nicole who shared the same birthday as my adopted father but different years of birth obviously.

Their was that squirrel again.

She shared with me that she had just gotten back from the historic Salem, Massachusetts. I told her I had gone in 2016. We shared photos.

The next morning the squirrel appeared again at breakfast

Then it was time to go home. This time the car was a giant broccoli. I thought okay let's go with it.

On the way home their were strange sightings beside the broccoli car which was strange enough. The road was blocked by a giant drumstick. Numbers had jumped off the exit signs and were floating around in the air.

Next three hot air balloons appeared before us. As we continued I saw more numbers had jumped off the exit signs.

31

Then two giant birds appeared out of nowhere.

Then a giant schnauzer was on the road.

Then upon arriving home Zoe the cat who was dumped by a breeder for being imperfect was waiting for me.

34

The perfect end to a perfect tournament.

The end.

36

Printed in the United States
by Baker & Taylor Publisher Services